Learning about
Insects and
Small Animals

by ROMOLA SHOWELL
with illustrations by RONALD LAMPITT

Ladybird Books Loughborough

What is an animal ?

Most of the living things in this world can be classified as either animals or plants. This book is about some of the smaller animals and how you can keep and observe them for short periods, before returning them to their natural environment (that is—where they usually live).

When we talk about animals we often mean things like dogs, cats, lions, tigers, etc., but these are only one group of animals called *mammals*. Mammals feed their young with milk. Mammals are also *vertebrates*— that is, they have a skull and internal skeleton of bones and cartilage covered with flesh and either skin or fur. There are other vertebrates that are not mammals. These include birds, fish, reptiles and amphibians.

Invertebrate animals—which means those having no bones—include all the insects, the worms, spiders, molluscs (such as snails and oysters), lobsters, crabs and many others. All these are interesting and worth studying.

If you are going to keep some of the small animals so that you can find out more about them, you will have to know something about their natural environment to be able to house them properly and know how to feed them. This book will help you. It will not tell you everything about the animals because so many things can be discovered by watching for yourself.

Keep a notebook and write down all that you see. You will find out a great deal about some of the animals that live around you.

These homes are NOT suitable

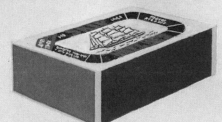

A match-box for a caterpillar

A traditional goldfish bowl

A weedless jam-jar for tadpoles

Stick insects

The common stick insects usually kept in schools are rather strange, wingless insects. They are natives of India. So many schools keep them that it is not difficult to obtain a few, or at least some eggs.

They are called stick insects because that is what they look like—greenish-brown sticks with six legs. When they are disturbed they fold up their legs and during the day can hardly be distinguished from bits of dry twig. They feed at night.

Any large jar or old fish tank will do to house these insects (when fully grown they are about 7 cm. long), but they must be kept supplied with fresh privet or ivy. This is best put into a small pot of water so that it does not dry up.

You can make your own cage out of a stout shoe-box. Cut a large rectangle in the lid and stick cellophane over it for an observation window, and then punch holes round the sides of the box for ventilation.

Your stick insect will moult several times during the six months before it is fully grown. The female can lay fertile eggs without a male being present, and continues to do so for a further seven or eight months, laying up to 500 eggs during its lifetime. Then the adult dies—by which time some of the eggs will have hatched. The eggs laid in the autumn usually hatch in late spring.

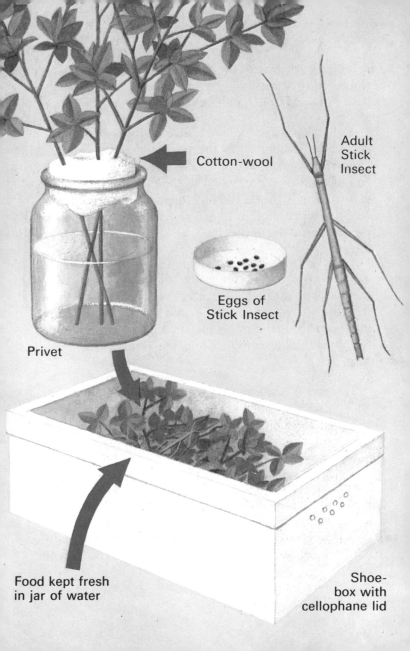

Cotton-wool

Adult
Stick
Insect

Eggs of
Stick Insect

Privet

Food kept fresh
in jar of water

Shoe-
box with
cellophane lid

Insects

Indian stick insects are unusual because they have no wings. Most insects have one or two pairs. They also have three pairs of legs and a pair of antennae, or feelers.

All insects have bodies that are divided into three parts. The front part is the head which has eyes and antennae (feelers), the middle is called the thorax (the legs and wings are attached to the thorax), and the rest of the body is called the abdomen. If you are not sure whether something you have caught is an insect, count the legs. If it has more than six legs, then it is not an insect.

A 'baby' insect is often not at all like the adult, and it has to pass through several changes in its life-cycle. Insects lay eggs which hatch into *larvae;* these change into *pupae* and the adult insects finally hatch out from the pupae. This complete change is called *metamorphosis*.

The eggs of the housefly are small, pointed and white, and the larvae, called maggots, hatch from them. After a while the maggots change to brown, barrel-shaped pupae, and inside the pupa case the maggot changes into the fly that we all know.

Some insects miss out the pupa stage. The mosquito is one of these, and so is the stick insect. It is difficult to tell the larva of a stick insect from the adult, except that it is smaller and sheds its skin periodically, so do not be surprised if you find dry, empty skins in your cage.

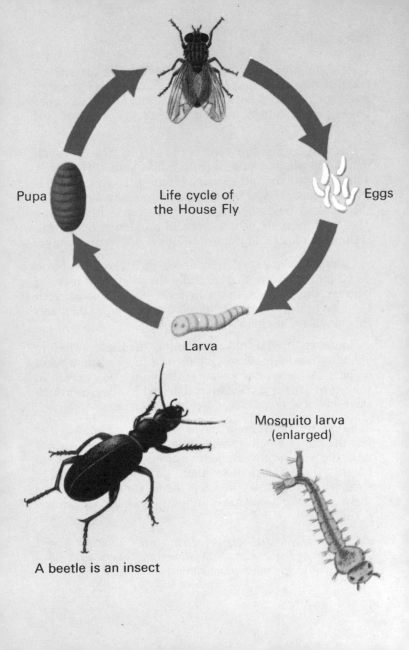

Pupa

Life cycle of
the House Fly

Eggs

Larva

Mosquito larva
(enlarged)

A beetle is an insect

Caterpillars

At some time you have probably found a caterpillar, taken it home and put it in a jar. Caterpillars are very interesting to keep because they are the larvae of either butterflies or moths, of which there are hundreds of different species.

Caterpillars are best kept in the sort of cage in which their food plants can be kept fresh in water. However, a large jar will do and so will a biscuit tin covered with a sheet of glass. If you use a biscuit tin, make air holes in the tin and bind the edges of the glass with sticking plaster or masking tape to prevent accidents. Better still is the cage illustrated opposite. This is not hard to make.

Caterpillars are very fussy about their food, so if you find a caterpillar, notice carefully the plant that it is on, because this may be its main food plant. Put in fresh food every day because caterpillars eat a great deal and they soon die if the leaves are dry.

Some caterpillars like to bury themselves before changing into pupae, so give them a layer of damp soil or peat. A piece of wood or bark should be inserted in the tin or jar for those caterpillars which like to attach themselves to fences, etc., before changing.

Watch for all the changes that take place and, when at last the pupae hatch (it may be in a week or two, or not until the next spring), look at your insects, use a book to identify them and then let them go. They will damage their wings if you try to keep them. Be sure to release them near the same trees or plants where you found them.

(*A few people are very sensitive to the hairs on 'furry' caterpillars. These hairs can sometimes cause a rash— so be careful when handling them.*)

10

Caterpillar of the
Large White Butterfly

Caterpillar of the
Magpie Moth

Caterpillar
cage

Air
holes

Glass
front to
wooden
box

Spare jar for fresh foliage to
which caterpillars can move

More about butterflies and moths

The eggs of butterflies and moths are laid on the food plant by the female insect and hatch into larvae or caterpillars.

Caterpillars spend their lives feeding and so grow very rapidly. The outer skin does not grow with the rest of the body and so has to be shed several times. When fully grown the larvae find a place to pupate. As mentioned on the previous page, many moth larvae bury themselves and some make themselves hard cases out of chewed up bark or wood. Some spin cocoons for themselves, and some just hang by fine threads from fences, etc. Inside the pupa case a marvellous change (metamorphosis) takes place.

If you look carefully at the pupa of the large white butterfly, you can see the outline of wings, antennae (feelers) and legs through the outer skin.

Butterflies and moths differ. Moths often have more unusual looking larvae, but the main differences can be seen in the adults. Most moths have fatter, hairy bodies and feathery antennae. Butterflies are more slender and their antennae are 'knobbed'. At rest a moth keeps its wings flat, but a butterfly folds them up at right angles to the body. Many moths fly only at night so a good place to look for them is round a street lamp on a warm, summer evening.

Few adults survive the winter, though some hibernate successfully. Pupae and also eggs can stay dormant until the spring.

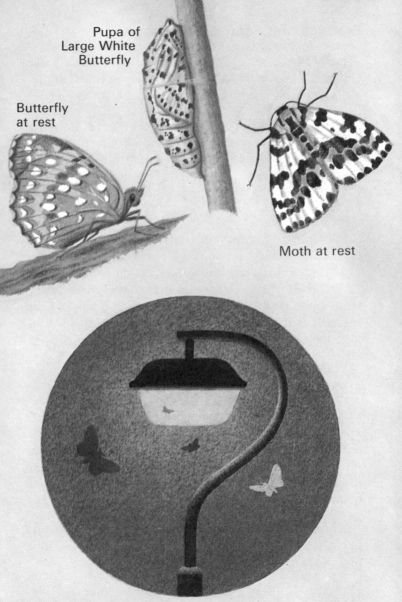

Pupa of Large White Butterfly

Butterfly at rest

Moth at rest

Moths flying round a street lamp

Earwigs, ants and woodlice

Earwigs and ants are insects, but woodlice are not. Count the legs to make sure. They can be found almost anywhere, and can be kept in quite small containers.

Woodlice like to spend most of their time in the dark, so look for them under stones or pieces of rotting wood. They can be kept in a shallow box, with a lid made of muslin or net held on with a rubber band. A wooden box is best, and damp leaves and stones should be put in it.

Earwigs will live quite happily between two pieces of inverted turf, and—if male and female are kept together—will lay eggs and rear young even in mid-winter. Do not be surprised if you see earwigs flying. Many can fly and their wings are usually kept hidden under a pair of wing cases. It is interesting, too, to know that earwigs look after their young after they have hatched from their eggs.

While you are studying earwigs, look for the pincers at the end of the abdomen.

A home for ants can be made from two pieces of glass and a framework of wood. The frame should be narrow and filled with a mixture of soil and sand. Holes drilled in two corners into which plastic tubing has been inserted can be used when feeding the ants on small quantities of jam or honey.

Ants need a certain amount of protein—and therefore in the wild eat small insects and larvae. They will soon pick a small bone clean.

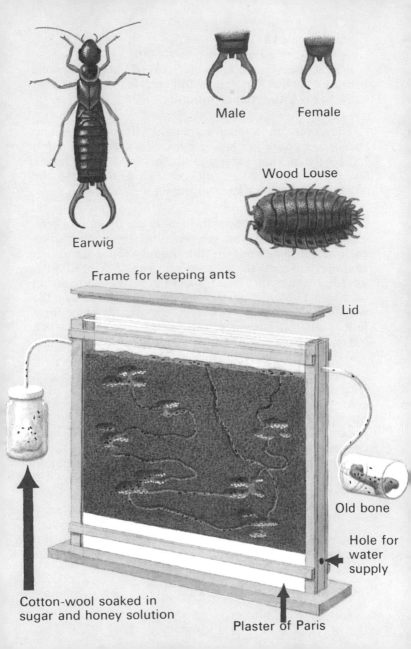

Male   Female

Wood Louse

Earwig

Frame for keeping ants

Lid

Cotton-wool soaked in
sugar and honey solution

Old bone

Hole for
water
supply

Plaster of Paris

Social insects

Wasps, bees and ants are called 'social' insects because they live in colonies and each insect has its own work to do within the community.

The queen ant is much larger than the other ants and spends her entire life laying eggs. She is fed and cared for by the worker ants, and these care for the larvae too. If you disturb an ant colony, you can see the workers carrying larvae and pupae to safety.

Most of the ant population is made up of workers. These are the ants you see scuttling about on garden paths and sometimes in the house. Occasionally in summer you may see a large number of winged ants. These are male ants and princess ants. They are flying off to start colonies of their own. After she has mated with a male, the princess ant finds a suitable place for a home, bites off her wings and begins laying eggs which hatch into workers for the new queen.

Ants will never form a real colony without a queen. You may be lucky and find one by digging out a colony, and if you do you can introduce her to her new home. An alternative construction which you can use for a colony is shown opposite. Hollows in the corners can be used for placing small quantities of jam, honey and small bones. If you drill a small hole as shown, and leave the box outside on a window sill, the workers will come and go as though it were a natural home. Once established, the queen will not leave.

Bees have a similar social life and you can find out more about them from the Ladybird book—'Life of the Honey Bee'.

Pupae

Worker Ants

Queen
Ant

Glass top to be covered
with black card

Tube inserted
for access

Ant colony with queen
in box on window sill

Spiders

Spiders belong to a family called the *Arachnids* and there are estimated to be 30,000 species of spider in the world. Some are poisonous to humans, but those that live in the British Isles are harmless.

A spider has a large abdomen and a head without feelers. It has eight legs, poison fangs and the number of eyes varies from four, six or eight, the majority of species having eight eyes.

Most spiders make webs. These are really traps for catching food. The spider builds its web where it is most likely to catch flies and then hides, coming out as soon as an insect gets caught in the web and paralysing it with a poison. Sometimes an insect is sucked dry of its life juices at once. Only when a spider's appetite is satisfied is the insect mummified and stored for a future occasion. Other spiders, like the wolf spider, go out hunting for food.

The web is produced from *spinnerets* at the end of the abdomen, and is incredibly fine and strong. A spider will let itself down on its web, and when it climbs back it loops the web up behind it with the back legs, and then discards this length of web at the end of the climb. A garden spider's web is called an orb web. A grass spider makes one that is funnel-shaped and one type makes a triangular web.

Some spiders live in water. They are air breathers so they have to collect air bubbles from the surface. An air bubble is usually carried down and held in place by the hairs of the underside of the abdomen and spinnerets, and then either absorbed into the body or into the silken bell—if one has been constructed. (See page 33.)

Common Garden Spider and newly hatched young

More about spiders

The common house spiders are the best to keep, though any other British spider will do.

The bigger the cage they are kept in the better, because if they have enough room they can spin their webs properly. It could be a box with a glass lid, but there also needs to be a hole (plugged with a cork or cotton wool) through which to feed the spiders. If you keep lifting the lid the webs will be broken.

A better cage is shown in the picture. This is made from two large tin lids, a sheet of acetate and a strip of Sellotape. Air holes are made in the lid, and a hole for feeding. You can see how to make it by looking at the picture.

Spiders like their food to be alive when it is caught in the web, so you will have to catch small flies for them. Catch them in a small jar and invert this over the hole in the lid. Sprinkle some spots of water through the hole occasionally.

If you find a cocoon of eggs or young spiders, put them in your 'spider house', though not with other large spiders. You can then see the young spiders moving up and down on their webs.

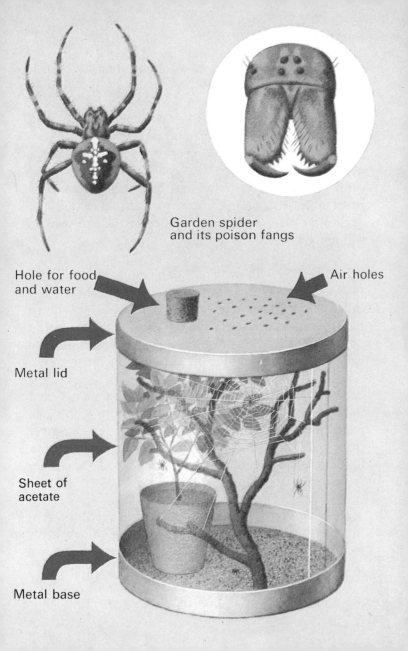

Garden spider
and its poison fangs

Hole for food
and water

Air holes

Metal lid

Sheet of
acetate

Metal base

Earthworms

Have you ever dug up a worm and then watched it wriggle away into the soil?

Earthworms are about the easiest animals to find, and you can dig them up in almost any garden. To keep them you will need a strong box—preferably wood—because the soil must be kept damp. Plywood or cardboard will soon be useless. You will need a glass panel in the front so that the worm-burrows can be seen against the glass. A lid is not needed because the worms will not get out.

Fill the box with ordinary, damp soil. This will also provide food. Worms feed on decaying plant matter, called *humus*, found in soil. If you want to see how much they move, put a layer of sand in the middle and notice how much it is disturbed. Some dead leaves on the top will be dragged in to plug the entrances of the burrows.

Put your worms on the top—not too many—and watch them disappear. Cover the glass front with black paper or cloth because worms automatically move away from light, and leave everything undisturbed for a few days. Then look under the cloth and you should see some of the worms against the glass.

Keep the soil damp and, if the worms are to be kept for some time, replace some of the soil with new every two or three weeks. Another type of wormery is shown opposite.

A wormery . Glass sides to be covered with black card so that the worms burrow against the glass

Glass edges bound with tape

Decaying leaves

Layer of sand

Earth

Pointed head

Worm in burrow

Flattened rear end

Fully-grown worm

More about soil animals

Worms feed on humus found in the soil and they lay their eggs in the soil. Their egg cocoons are not easy to see because they are small, round and brown. The best place to look for them is in a good compost heap where tiny worms can often be seen hatching.

Worms move by extending the front of their bodies and then drawing up the back part. If you measure a worm that is stretched out, it is considerably longer than when it is relaxed. Put a worm on a piece of paper and listen to it moving. The tiny rustling sound is caused by pairs of bristles on the underside.

Dig in a garden and you may find other invertebrates. We have already mentioned the pupae of some moths, but you may find the grubs (larvae) of beetles such as the cockchafer, and also millipedes and centipedes.

Centipede means 'hundred footed', but the number of their feet varies considerably. You will be able to see that the body is made up of segments. The centipede has one pair of legs on each segment. The millipede has two pairs on each segment. Most centipedes are surface feeders and are carnivorous, whereas millipedes are generally vegetarians. If you are keeping some to look at, put some damp leaves with them because they soon die in dry air.

Centipede

Millipede

Segment of millipede

Segment of centipede

Larva of Cockchafer Beetle

Pupa of the Privet Hawk Moth in soil

Snails

Like worms, snails are invertebrates, but they have a shell to protect them and can completely withdraw into it. They also have feelers, and eyes on the end of 'stalks'. To find snails, look in between the stones of old walls, under damp stones and on the undersides of leaves.

Snails can be kept in almost any large wooden box, using a sheet of glass, or fine mesh netting on a frame, for a lid.

Put a good layer of damp soil on the bottom, and several stones. Arrange some of these so that the snails can get underneath them. Keep the whole thing in a cool, shady place, particularly if you are using a glass cover.

Snails will eat any fresh, green leaves. Remove any that are uneaten each day and replace with new ones. Snails will do most of their feeding at night, so see that the food is left overnight.

Keep the soil moist and the snails will live for a long time. If they are kept under good conditions, and are fed regularly, they will lay eggs in the summer. These are laid in hollows in damp soil in clusters of about 20-40. After a few weeks or a few months (depending on the time of year when laid), the eggs will hatch into tiny snails, perfect miniatures of the adults. They will spend most of their time eating, and will soon grow.

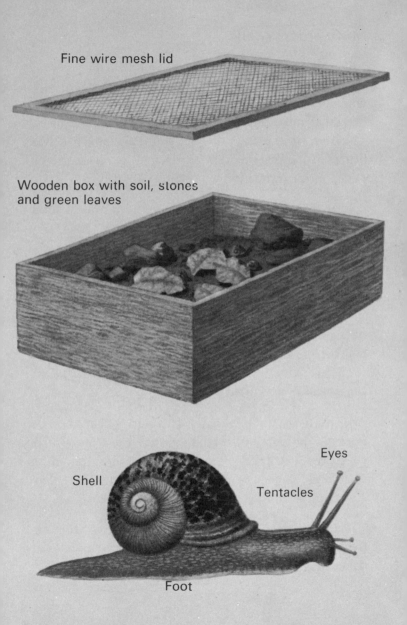

Fine wire mesh lid

Wooden box with soil, stones and green leaves

Shell

Eyes

Tentacles

Foot

More about snails

If one of your snails refuses to come out of its shell, dip it quickly into slightly warmed water and it will gradually appear. You will see the soft body and the breathing hole, where the body joins the spiral shell. The eyes, on the ends of long tentacles, look like two black dots. Touch one very gently, and see how it can be pulled in for protection.

It is difficult to see a snail's mouth, but put it on a piece of glass and look from underneath. It is also possible to hear a snail feeding because it scrapes away at leaves with its rough, file-like tongue. This tongue consists of rows of tiny teeth, and it keeps growing to replace the wear of constant eating.

The snail can be watched as it moves across the glass, and the muscles can be seen rippling along the body. It travels smoothly on a layer of slime. This is what causes the silvery 'snail's trails'.

In winter snails hibernate. This means that they lie dormant throughout the cold weather when food would be scarce. They find sheltered places, withdraw into their shells and seal the openings with dried slime. There they stay until the spring.

There are several species of snail. The commonest is the large brown garden snail. There are also pond and sea snails.

Mouth

Looking at the underneath of a snail through glass

Snail hibernating in soil

Look under leaves for snails

Water snails

Pond snails are simple to keep, but there is no easy way of making a home for pond creatures. A proper aquarium tank is really the only thing, but once it is set up it can be used to house a whole variety of different plants and animals. Plastic tanks are cheaper than glass ones, but the largest you can get will be the best in the end.

Having obtained a tank, put it in position while empty (water is heavy and a full tank is hard to move). It will have to be in a good light for the weed to thrive. Cover the bottom with sand and several clean stones. Make a corner with larger stones so that you can plant some weed.

The water weed is absolutely essential. It is this which provides oxygen and also serves as food for some animals. If you happen to know of a pond or stream where you can find weed, you can also look for snails and such things as water shrimps.

Plant the weed in soil in the corner where you put the larger stones and then cover the soil with smaller stones. If your tank is a big one, you could also have a small rush or peppermint plant growing in a plastic pot in another corner. This will grow up above the water. These plants can be found at the edges of ponds or streams if you are lucky enough to live near either of these.

Fill the tank with water—poured on to a sheet of stiff paper to avoid disturbing the sand, and leave it for a few days before putting any animals in it.

Aquarium tank

Light should come from one direction only

When filling, pour the water onto a sheet of stiff paper

More about pond life

There are two main types of water snail—the ramshorn snail and the great pond snail, and both will live happily in an aquarium tank. Avoid having too many because they feed on the plants. Also, if you have sufficient plants, it should never be necessary to empty the tank, but just to top it up with water.

While pond hunting you may find fish, frogs and fresh water mussels, but there are also many smaller things that you can catch to put in your tank.

Caddis fly larvae are some of the more curious. They make themselves little tubes out of bits of twig or small stones. Only the head and legs stick out of the tube. They can be found crawling along the bottom of shallow ponds and streams.

On the surface, pond skaters and water boatmen may be found. The water boatman only comes to the surface to thrust the tip of its abdomen (which is covered with a tuft of bristles) through the surface film to re-plenish its air supply. It then swims down to anchor itself on a plant. Pond skaters and water boatmen do not often live away from their natural homes. If you are very lucky you may find one of the water spiders we mentioned earlier, and this will live quite happily in a tank with a good supply of weed, but it will feed on any small tadpoles and water shrimps.

If you look carefully at a jar of pond water, you can see tiny living things shooting about. These will probably be water fleas or cyclops. Try and look at these under a microscope or strong magnifying glass. A microscope will show you many other things too: perhaps a hydra or mosquito larvae. With pond life there is always something new to watch.

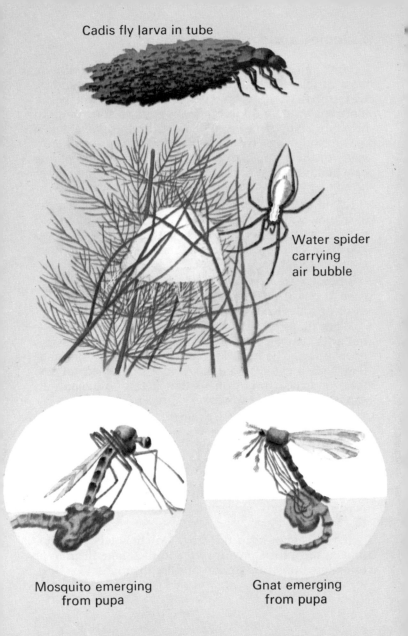

Cadis fly larva in tube

Water spider carrying air bubble

Mosquito emerging from pupa

Gnat emerging from pupa

Tadpoles and frogs

Most children know what frog spawn looks like—a mass of jelly-like eggs which soon hatch into tadpoles. Unfortunately, it is a fact that soon there will be no more spawn or tadpoles unless we all do something to help preserve them. For years collectors have taken spawn and frogs from ponds and streams, and now many of these ponds are being filled in when preparing new building sites, so that the frogs have fewer and fewer breeding places.

If you are lucky enough to find frog spawn—usually in shallow water—take about twelve eggs only and leave the rest where they can hatch naturally. The few eggs you have taken will be quite enough for you to take home or to school.

Tadpoles are best kept in the sort of tank shown on page 31 but, if this is not possible, make a mini-tank for three or four. Keep it out of the hot sun.

When they first hatch they will feed off the spawn jelly, but after that they will need pond weed until their legs have grown. The back legs grow first, and at this stage they need a change of diet. A very small piece of raw meat (attached to cotton so that it can be pulled out) can be put into the tank for a short time.

As soon as the front legs grow, the tadpoles need to be able to get out of the water and will need a large stone or floating raft for this.

If you have a proper vivarium at school (like that in the picture) you can keep frogs. The bottom is covered with turf, and there is a sunken dish of water. For food they need small worms, slugs and insects, or may even refuse to eat at all.

If you cannot keep the frogs—or they will not eat—look at them for a day or two and then take them to an unpolluted pond or stream and let them go.

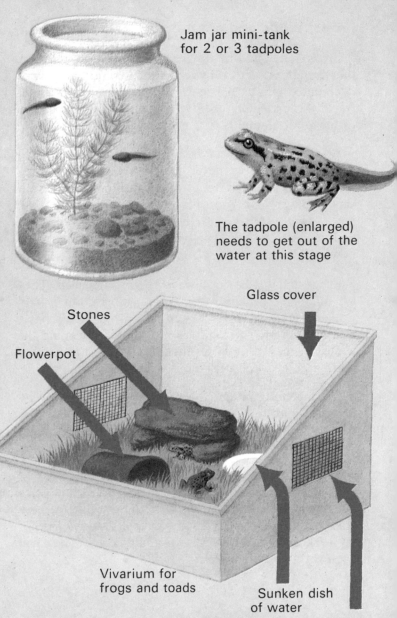

Jam jar mini-tank for 2 or 3 tadpoles

The tadpole (enlarged) needs to get out of the water at this stage

Glass cover

Stones

Flowerpot

Vivarium for frogs and toads

Sunken dish of water

Ventilation

Frogs, toads and newts

Frogs, toads and newts are amphibians. This means they spend part of their lives in water, as well as on land. Each one begins as an egg which hatches into a tadpole. As in the insect life-history, the change from tadpole to the adult animal is called metamorphosis.

All these creatures can be kept in a vivarium, but the toads will probably never go near the water. They prefer to hide under stones in a damp corner, or in a small flower pot (not plastic) turned on its side. Newts usually only go into the water when they are adult and ready to mate. They will then need a very large bowl.

Frogs and toads can always be distinguished. They are different in many ways. A frog jumps, but a toad walks; a toad has a dry, rough skin, while a frog has a wet, smooth one; a frog lives near water, spending the winter in the wet mud of ditches, but a toad will only go to a pond for egg-laying.

All three feed on the same sort of food and, if you are not too squeamish, it is fascinating to see how a frog eats a worm. The normal food is flies. These are caught by a hinged, sticky tongue which flicks out and catches insects several inches away.

Toad and frog tadpoles are similar, but newt tadpoles are dainty, semi-transparent little things with feathery gills and tiny, trailing legs. A warning, though! Do not try to keep any tadpoles with adult newts. They will soon eat up any tadpoles.

Common Toad

Common Frog

Smooth Newt, eggs and tadpole (enlarged)

Minnows and sticklebacks

Minnows and sticklebacks, if you are lucky enough to find them, are best kept in an outdoor pond—but not together. Sticklebacks will attack any other fish. It is quite easy to see the difference between minnows and sticklebacks because the sharp spines along the back of the stickleback are obvious.

You will need some help to make an outdoor pond and your teacher will probably help you to make one using a large sheet of polythene (it has to be the proper sort for ponds or it will tear) or you may have an old sink which can be used. In this pond you can also keep water shrimps, caddis, snails and water beetles as well as the essential pond plants.

If you want to study fish but cannot obtain minnows or sticklebacks, you could keep small goldfish in a tank instead. These will have to be bought but they will live a long time in a well-kept aquarium. Fish are often given far too much food, and any uneaten food rots, fouls the water, and the fish die. A pinch of food, bought from pet shops, given every other day is enough for two small fish. The best sort is called 'Dried Daphnia'.

The ordinary round goldfish bowl is not suitable. It is too small and the top opening lets in insufficient air to the surface of the water. If you have one of these bowls use it for caterpillars, instead!

Remember—a good aquarium needs plenty of green weed.

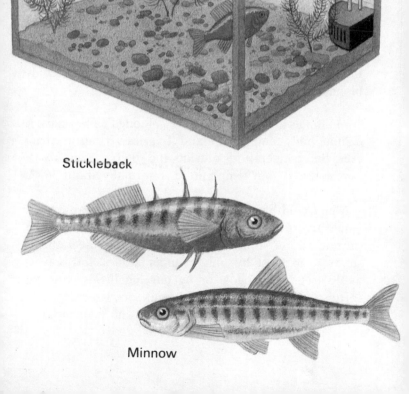

Tank with electric pump for aeration

Stickleback

Minnow

Cold or warm blooded ?

It is fascinating to watch a fish swimming. The smooth, silent movement through the water looks so effortless. If you watch, you will see how the side-to-side curving of the body propels it along, and how the fins and tail are used for changing direction, or moving up and down.

A fish looks as if it is drinking all the time, but the continual opening and shutting of its mouth is to take in water which passes over the gills and out from under the gill-covers at the side of the head. As the water goes over the gills, oxygen is absorbed by the blood. Land animals get their oxygen from the air.

Fish, like the amphibians, are cold-blooded. This means that they have a temperature the same as that of the air or water around them. Reptiles are also cold-blooded.

Mammals and birds are 'warm-blooded'. They have a definite body temperature and it varies very little whatever the temperature outside the body. You are a mammal and your temperature is normally about 36°C.

Many cold-blooded animals hibernate because they would freeze if their temperature altered to that of the outside air on some winter days. They protect themselves from frost by hiding under stones and leaves, as do frogs and toads, or by burying themselves like tortoises. Snails hibernate too, and so do some warm-blooded mammals such as field mice and hedgehogs.

Movement of a fish

Water goes in

Gill cover

Water passes out
over the gills

Tortoises and grass snakes

Tortoises and grass snakes are reptiles and both can be kept without much difficulty. The type of tortoises we buy in this country are called Greek tortoises. They come from countries that are warmer and drier than ours, so they need to be protected from cold and damp. It is the wet more than the cold that kills most of them.

A tortoise is best kept outside in a large run which can be made of wood or wire-netting on a frame. It need not be very high because a tortoise cannot climb. One corner can be covered with a board to make a shelter. The tortoise needs fresh food every day: dandelions, lettuce, cabbage, groundsel, tomato, apple—and plenty of water. The water bowl should be sunk into the ground so that the tortoise can get its head into it. In the late summer it must be taken in at night, and as soon as it shows signs of trying to hibernate, it should be put in a box lined with newspaper and filled with dry leaves. Leave in a cool, dry place for the winter.

A grass snake can be kept in an old aquarium tank with a lid made of very fine mesh netting on a frame. Line the bottom with soil and stones and put in a climbing branch. A bowl of water is also needed. Never underestimate the strength of a snake. It will be necessary to put a stone on the lid or the snake will escape. Feed a grass snake on small worms, slugs, maggots and large flies. It is a difficult creature to keep because it is often so alarmed that it will refuse to eat for the first few days. *If* a snake is kept, this should be for a day or two only—after which it should be returned to its place of capture.

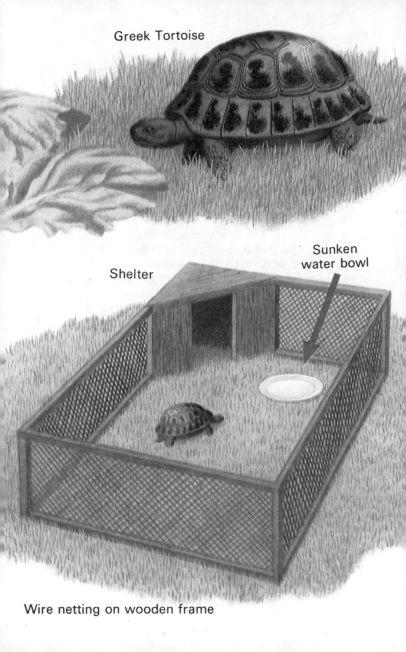

Greek Tortoise

Shelter

Sunken water bowl

Wire netting on wooden frame

More about reptiles

Most people seem to be afraid of touching snakes. They expect them to be cold and slimy, but they are quite dry and as warm as the air around them. They are extremely strong and muscular, and will wrap themselves round your arm or hold themselves out quite straight like a piece of stick. The grass snake is quite harmless and it can be distinguished from our other native snake, the adder, by the V-shaped marking behind the adder's head. *Never* try to capture an adder.

The adder is poisonous. It has poison sacs which open into the two hollow fangs. It has to bite to poison its victim. The forked tongue which flicks in and out is just a tongue, and that's all! A snake moves by using its very powerful muscles and these muscles curve it from side to side. It can move very rapidly indeed.

The slow worm looks like a snake but is really a lizard. Ordinary small lizards are quite common in the south of England and can be seen basking on rocks on warm days, but they move so quickly that they are hard to spot.

If you find a slow worm or lizard, keep it for a few days only and then let it go in the place where you found it. It is interesting to note here that a frightened lizard will try to escape from its captor by shedding the end of its tail. This is left, still moving, while the lizard runs away (it will grow a new one in time).

All the reptiles lay eggs—round ones with leathery shells. Sometimes a newly bought tortoise will lay a batch of eggs in a hole in the garden, but these very rarely hatch even when kept somewhere warm.

Common Lizard

Grass Snake

Head of Adder, or Viper

Mice

Mice are small mammals and can be kept without much expense. One or two can be kept in a cage and they are pretty little things to watch. There are many different colourings and markings. Two females will live together quite happily, but two males tend to fight. If you keep a pair you will be able to watch the babies growing up, but mice have up to eight babies at a time and will produce a new litter every few weeks.

If you like carpentry, make your own cage. It will be cheaper than a bought one and perhaps you can persuade an adult to help. A wooden cage is best, with a door made of glass in a wooden frame. Air holes will have to be drilled in the sides of the cage. To make the whole thing more interesting, a shelf can be put inside with a slope or ladder going up to it. One corner needs partitioning off so the mice can make a nest. If the floor is kept covered with sawdust or dry peat and cleaned regularly, the mice will not smell. The nest can be made of hay, material, etc.

Mice need water and a method of giving them a constant supply is shown in the picture. They feed on seeds, oats, cornflakes, raisins, baked bread, etc.

The same cage can be used for hamsters or gerbils, but these will have to be watched as they can chew through thin wood very quickly.

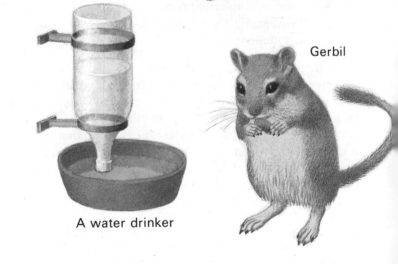

Mouse cage
with glass front

Mesh, or drilled holes,
for ventilation

A water drinker

Gerbil

Mammals

Most of the pets we keep are mammals—cats, dogs, rabbits, guinea pigs, hamsters.

Mammals are animals that feed their young on milk from their own bodies. In most cases an egg is not laid, the baby animal growing inside the mother until it is ready to be born. Baby mammals that are born in nests, like rabbits, mice and hamsters, are quite helpless when they are born and often have no hair at all. They need to be looked after by the mother for quite a long time. Other mammals, like cows, horses and sheep, are born outside and have a good covering of hair. They can move about almost immediately.

Mammals are also warm blooded and the fully grown ones have a covering of hair or fur to keep in the warmth (except human beings who have to wear clothes, instead).

If you keep any animal as a pet, remember that it will need a proper cage, the right food, water and protection from the weather. Find out how to look after an animal before you actually buy it.

On the whole, small mammals do not live very long. Hamsters, mice and gerbils live for 2-3 years, and guinea pigs about 4 years. However, cats, dogs and rabbits can live for 8-10 years or more, so make sure that you are prepared to look after them for all that time. It is too easy to forget that the pretty baby stage does not last very long, and that all animals need a lot of care. Once caged—they are dependent on *you* for food, water and the right living conditions.

Mother cat feeding kittens

Most mammals are covered with hair or fur

What can we find out?

If you keep a notebook and write down all the things that you observe about animals, you will learn more than if you had just read about them in books. Use books, of course, but use them to add to your own findings and to help you with identification.

What can be found out about the animals you keep? Perhaps these questions will help you to make a start.

What is it?
How big is it?
Where is it found?
What colour is it, and has it any body covering?
What shape is the body?
Has it any legs? How many?
How does it move?
Has it got feelers?
Has it got eyes?
What does it feed on?
Does it lay eggs?
Does it change—other than in size—as it grows?
Does it make any sound?
Is there anything else to be discovered?

Can you draw? What about a collection of drawings; or photographs if you are a photographer?

Whatever you do, you will realise how interesting the smallest animal can be, and you will have learned something about the wonderful variety of life that is to be found all around us, everywhere.

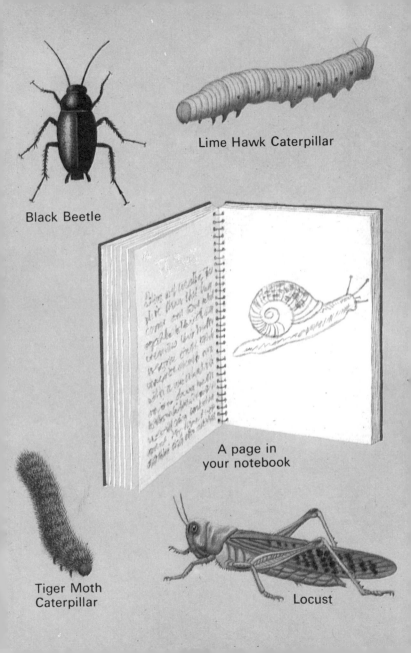

Black Beetle

Lime Hawk Caterpillar

A page in
your notebook

Tiger Moth
Caterpillar

Locust

Series 651
A Ladybird Natural History Book